First published 1985 by
Deans International Publishing
Copyright © 1985 Victoria House Publishing Ltd.
This edition published 1989 by
Colour Library Books Ltd,
Godalming, Surrey, England.
ISBN 0 86283 661 1
All rights reserved

Printed in the German Democratic Republic

LITTLE BUNNY'S
BEDTIME STORIES

Written by Lis Taylor
Illustrated by Colin Petty

Colour Library Books

Contents

LITTLE
BUNNY'S
BEDTIME
STORIES

The Babysitter

Mr and Mrs Bunny were going out for the evening to a party, and Little Bunny's brother, Benny, was staying with a friend.

"But we don't *need* a babysitter," complained Little Bunny.

"Yes you do," said Mr Bunny, firmly. "There's more to looking after Bunnykins than you think. And Mrs Badger is coming to sit with you."

Little Bunny pouted. And he carried on pouting even when Mrs Badger had arrived.

"I could look after Bunnykins on my own," he said, when his mummy and daddy had left.

"All right," said Mrs Badger, "you can!" And she took out her knitting.

Just then, Little Bunny heard a noise from the bedroom, so off he ran to see what Bunnykins wanted.

"Whaaah!" went Bunnykins, who was just learning to talk. "Drink!"

8

Little Bunny dashed to the kitchen to fetch her a drink, which Mummy had left in a flask. Bunnykins carried on crying, "Whaaah!"

Little Bunny carried the drink carefully back to Bunnykins and helped her to finish it up. Then he tucked the blankets all round

her again and tiptoed out of the room. But just as he got to the door he heard, "Whaaah!" again.

"Hot!" cried Bunnykins, wriggling in her cot. "Too hot!"

Little Bunny carefully took off a blanket, and tucked her in again.

When there was no more noise from the cot, Little Bunny went back to sit with Mrs Badger. He wanted to look at his comic. He'd only just sat down when, "Whaaah!" came again from the bedroom.

"Oh, no!" groaned Little Bunny.

But Mrs Badger just smiled in a comfortable way and carried on with her knitting.

When Little Bunny reached the bedroom, he found Bunnykins sitting up in her cot, crying.

"Can't sleep!" she wailed.

So Little Bunny began to sing. He sang Bunnykins four songs which Mr Mole had taught them at school—but she didn't go to sleep. Then he tried some nursery rhymes, and by the time he'd got to Humpty Dumpty he was feeling quite tired himself!

"Story!" yelled Bunnykins, when he'd finished.

At that moment Little Bunny was very pleased to see Mrs Badger coming into the bedroom with a storybook in her hand.

"Here you are," she said. "Quiet now, and I'll read you both a story." And she did.

When she'd finished, Mrs Badger turned to Little Bunny.

"So you found babysitting hard work after all?" she asked.

But Little Bunny didn't hear her. He was fast asleep!

The Tea Cosy

"Is there any more tea in the pot?" asked Mr Squirrel.

"Yes," said Mrs Squirrel, having a look, "but I think it's a bit cold."

"We need a tea cosy," said Mr Squirrel.

"What a good idea!" agreed Little Squirrel.

She had just learned to knit and had been wondering what she could make for Christmas. Now she knew. She chose some bright red wool from her work basket and started to knit.

It took her quite a long time, but she finished it on Christmas Eve, wrapped it and put it under the tree.

On Christmas morning Little Squirrel was up early.

"Please can we open our presents before breakfast?" she asked. Mr Squirrel shook his head.

"We always have breakfast first," he said, giving her a hug.

11

"What's the hurry this year?"

"Could you open just one of your presents, then?" she asked. "It's for a special reason."

"All right," said Mrs Squirrel, laughing. "I'll just put the kettle on."

Little Squirrel brought their present into the kitchen and Mr Squirrel unwrapped it.

"It's a—a cushion!" he said. He put it on his chair and sat down.

"No, no!" laughed Mrs Squirrel. "It isn't a cushion, it's just what we needed—a tea cosy! Clever Little Squirrel to knit one."

Mrs Squirrel poured water into the teapot and then took the cosy and popped it on. There was a hole for the handle so she slipped the handle through and then tried to push the spout through its hole. It wouldn't go.

"Let's try it the other way round," she said.

But, no matter how she tried, she couldn't get both the handle and the spout through their holes. Poor Little Squirrel looked very disappointed.

"The holes are too close together, aren't they?" she said.

Just then there was a knock at the door. It was Little Bunny with a Christmas present for Little Squirrel.

"Happy Christmas!" he called, running to the kitchen fire to warm his paws. "It's frosty out there this morning. I wish I'd worn a hat," and he rubbed his head.

"*I've* got a hat for you," said Little Squirrel, holding up the tea cosy.

Little Bunny tried it on and it fitted perfectly. The holes were in just the right places for his ears!

"Well done, Little Squirrel!" said Mr Squirrel. "I know!" he added. "Why don't we use that old hat of mine with all the holes in as a tea cosy?" And that is what they did!

Mr Bunny's Secret

Mr Bunny had just finished building a new garden wall when Little Bunny and Benny arrived home from school.

"The wall looks great, Dad," said Benny. "But what will you do with all the left-over bricks and sand?"

"I'll think of something," said Mr Bunny. "What did you two do at school today?"

"We talked about the seaside," said Little Bunny. "Mr Mole said we might go there one day on a school trip. I want to take my bucket and spade so I can build a sandcastle...."

"That's it!" shouted Mr Bunny, suddenly.

"What?" they both asked.

But Mr Bunny wouldn't say. He loaded all the spare bricks into a wheelbarrow, and disappeared down the road. Then he came back to fetch the sand and the cement.

"I wonder where he's taking it all?" asked Benny.

The next day was Saturday. Mr Bunny went out early in the morning and nobody knew where he had gone. At least, if Mrs

14

Bunny knew, she didn't tell Benny and Little Bunny.

When they arrived at school on Monday morning everyone was in the playground and there was a lot of chattering.

"Where did it come from?" asked Little Owl.

"Do you think we can play in it now?" asked Little Squirrel.

Little Bunny and Benny ran up to the crowd in the playground to find out why everyone was so excited. They stood on tiptoe to look over all the heads and ears—and there they saw a beautiful new sandpit.

They smiled at each other. "So that's what our daddy was doing!" said Little Bunny, proudly.

The Lookalikes

Cousin Katie had come to stay with Little Squirrel.

"Well, well," said Mrs Squirrel, looking at the two cousins, "you two are almost like twin squirrels!"

It was true. When they both looked in the mirror they could hardly tell the difference themselves! Their noses, their eyes and their long bushy tails were almost identical.

"I think we could have some fun," said Little Squirrel to Katie. "Let's play a trick on my friends," and she whispered her plan into Katie's ear.

Later that afternoon, in the wood, Little Squirrel sent Katie to hide behind a tree and went to join the others in their game of hide-and-seek.

Soon it was Little Squirrel's turn to hide. She left her friends counting to ten and ran off to hide behind a tree on the opposite side of the clearing from Katie. Then, as planned, Katie jumped out and waved. "Here I am!" she called. Everyone ran towards her.

A minute later, from the other tree, out popped Little Squirrel. "No—over here!" she cried.

The friends turned around in amazement. How could Little Squirrel be in *two* places at once?

By this time, Katie had dashed to another hiding place, and she poked her head around the tree trunk, calling, "Yoo hoo, here I am!"

Everyone looked very puzzled. "Just how many Little Squirrels are there today?" asked Little Mouse, quite confused.

"Only one!" laughed Little Squirrel, as she ran over to them. "This is my cousin Katie who looks just like me."

Everyone thought it was a good joke, but they all agreed with Benny Bunny that *one* Little Squirrel was quite enough!

Little Bunny Washes Up

One day Little Bunny asked his mummy if he could help her with the housework. Mrs Bunny was very pleased that Little Bunny wanted to help and she gave him a tiny brush so that he could sweep alongside her.

After a while, Mrs Bunny went over to the window and looked out. She said, "There's Mrs Squirrel coming along the path. I'll just pop out for a chat, Little Bunny. You can help me wash the

dishes when I come back." And out she went.

Little Bunny thought to himself, "I will wash the dishes all on my own. That will be a surprise for Mummy!"

Fetching a stool from under the kitchen table, Little Bunny stood on it so he could reach the taps.

First he squeezed the washing-up liquid into the bowl. He wasn't sure just how much to squeeze in, so he added a bit more—and then more again. When he thought it was enough, he turned both taps on full. As the water spurted into the bowl, the washing-up liquid turned into hundreds of tiny bubbles.

They spilled over the bowl and onto the floor, and even started to cover the stool that Little Bunny was standing on before he could manage to turn off the taps!

"Oh no!" cried Little Bunny. What am I going to do? Mummy will be really cross—the kitchen is all bubbly!"

Then he had an idea.

He opened the window above the sink. Then he went to the door leading to the garden and opened that too. This made a breeze and the bubbles began to rise and drift out of the window.

Mrs Bunny was still talking to Mrs Squirrel when she suddenly saw a strange sight above her house. "Look!" she said, pointing to the sky, "hundreds of bubbles with the sun shining on them! I wonder where they came from?"

They watched the bubbles float like a cloud and then scatter in the air.

By the time Mrs Bunny had said good-bye to Mrs Squirrel, Little Bunny had everything in the kitchen back to normal. What a narrow escape!

"Are you ready to help me with the washing-up, now?" asked Mrs Bunny.

Little Bunny just smiled and nodded his head slowly, as one, last, tiny bubble glistened on the end of his whiskers.

The School Photograph

"This afternoon I'm going to take a photograph of you all," said Mr Mole, "so make sure you're looking neat and tidy."

The class was rather excited all morning at the thought of this. Little Owl was particularly excited, so much so that he kept talking when he was supposed to be doing his sums and giggling when Mr Mole turned to the blackboard.

Mr Mole began to get rather cross with Little Owl.

"If I turn round once more and find you giggling, you won't be in the school photograph," he warned.

But Little Owl still giggled and when it was time for the photograph Mr Mole told him to stay in the classroom.

"Everyone else please line up in the playground," he said.

It took Mr Mole a long time to get everyone arranged. When, at last, he was happy with the way they were standing he had to fiddle with his camera to get the picture just right.

He peered through it and shouted, "I can't get you all in. Will the ones at the sides move in a bit?"

Everyone sighed as they moved yet again.

Inside the classroom, Little Owl was feeling very sorry for

20

himself. What would Mr and Mrs Owl say when they found out he wasn't in the school photograph? Then he'd be in trouble!

He wandered round the classroom thinking about what would happen. He stopped for a moment by Mr Mole's desk and noticed a roll of film lying there.

"Oh no!" thought Little Owl. "He's taking the school photograph without any film in the camera!"

He grabbed the film and dashed into the playground as Mr Mole was saying, "Thank you. You can all go now."

"No!" shouted Little Owl. "Stop! Stay where you are!"

"What are you doing out here?" asked Mr Mole, crossly.

But when Little Owl explained and handed him the film Mr Mole was very pleased.

"Thank you, Little Owl. It's a good thing you came to tell me. I think that you deserve to be in the photograph after all."

So Little Owl took his place with the others and beamed all over his face!

Little Bunny is Ill

One morning when Little Bunny came down for breakfast Mrs Bunny sent him straight back up to bed.

"You don't look well enough for school today," she told him. "I'll call Doctor Hare to have a look at you."

"Oh dear," said Doctor Hare, peering seriously at Little Bunny over his glasses. "I'm afraid you'll have to stay in bed, young bunny—for three days at least. And he's to take this medicine every hour, Mrs Bunny. Make sure he doesn't miss it."

Poor Little Bunny was soon bored. He had read all his books, drawn pictures on every piece of paper in the house and done all his jigsaws at least twice. What was worse, the medicine he had to take tasted horrible and he dreaded the clock chiming the hour because he knew his mummy would arrive with another spoonful.

Just then there was a knock on the door. It was Little Owl.

"I'm sorry to hear about Little Bunny," he said. "I've brought him some grapes. May I go up and see him?"

"Yes of course. He'll be very pleased to see you," said Mrs Bunny.

There was another knock on the door. This time it was Little Squirrel with a big bag of tangerines. She went up to see Little Bunny, too.

Then Nippy Shrew arrived and Percy Woodpecker and several more friends. They all brought Little Bunny oranges or apples or grapes and they all stayed to play.

At bedtime, when they had all gone home, Little Bunny was much more cheerful.

"They're going to come and see me every day," he told Mrs Bunny, "so I won't be bored at all. If only I didn't have to take that horrid medicine it wouldn't be so bad staying in bed."

Mrs Bunny looked at the huge bowl of fruit beside Little Bunny's bed.

"I know!" she said. "Every time you have a spoonful of medicine you can have a piece of fruit afterwards to help get rid of the taste."

After that, Little Bunny so looked forward to his apple or orange that he didn't really mind having to take his medicine!

Ricky Fox Makes Friends

There were some newcomers to Hollyholt. Mr and Mrs Fox had just moved in, with their son Ricky.

"My goodness," said Mrs Fox, looking at all the boxes as they were unloaded. "I didn't realise we had so many things."

One by one, the boxes were unpacked and Mrs Fox put the empty ones in the front garden. There just wasn't room for them anywhere else.

"Would you like to play with them?" she asked Ricky.

"What can I do with a lot of old boxes?" he asked.

"You could make a train from them," said his mummy.

So Ricky wandered outside and spent the rest of the morning by himself in the garden. He piled up all the boxes to make an engine, with a chain of trucks behind.

"This would be much more fun if I had someone to play with," he told his mummy, when she came to call him inside for lunch.

"You'll soon make friends, Ricky," she said. "You will be starting school on Monday, and you'll get to know everyone there."

Ricky knew this was true but he wished he didn't have to spend the whole weekend on his own until Monday morning came.

After lunch, Ricky went outside again to carry on with his game. Soon, Little Squirrel and Little Mouse came along and caught sight of Ricky's fine train.

"Oh, that looks great," said Little Squirrel. "Did you build it yourself?"

Well, that was all Ricky needed! Before long, both Little Squirrel and Little Mouse were sitting in the trucks, and Ricky was pretending to drive them in his 'engine'.

Then Little Bunny, Benny and Little Owl came by, and joined in the fun. Mrs Fox *was* pleased when she looked out of the window—it seemed as if half of Ricky's class were playing with him in the garden.

As Mrs Fox tucked Ricky into bed that night she smiled as she said, "Those boxes came in useful after all, didn't they, Ricky?"

"Yes," yawned Ricky, "and tomorrow we're going to make them into a spaceship!"

Little Bunny Learns to Fly

Little Owl and Little Bunny were playing trains in the school playground.

"I'm bored," said Little Bunny. "Let's play aeroplanes instead."

"Great!" said Little Owl. He took off, flew round the playground making aeroplane noises and landed beside Little Bunny.

"It's not fair," moaned Little Bunny. "I can't fly." He thought for a moment and then said, "Do you think you could teach me?"

"It's easy!" answered Little Owl. "But you haven't any wings."

"No problem," said Little Bunny, sounding very sure. "I can make some wings. We'll have a grand take-off on Saturday!"

Little Bunny was so excited at the idea of flying that he told everyone. "Come and see me fly," he boasted. "The first airborne bunny! I'll be making history!"

When Saturday came there was quite a crowd gathered at the foot of the Owls' tree. Little Owl helped Little Bunny to put on his wings. They were made from twigs and feathers.

"I'm not sure they'll work," said Little Owl, shaking his head.

"Yours do," said Little Bunny. "Why shouldn't mine?"

He bowed proudly to the crowd who all cheered and shouted, "Come on, Little Bunny." Then he took up his position.

"Ready, steady, go!" called Little Owl and off ran Little Bunny as hard as he could, flapping his feathery arms madly.

"If only I could flap just a tiny bit harder, I'm *sure* it would

work," he told himself. He closed his eyes and tried to imagine that he was soaring higher and higher above the trees out into the clear blue sky. . . . Suddenly, THUMP!

When Little Bunny opened his eyes again he was lying on his back under a huge oak tree and his head ached. Little Owl was bending over him.

"Did I do it?" Little Bunny whispered, thinking he must have fallen from the sky.

"No," said Little Owl, sadly. "You ran into a tree!"

"Oh dear," groaned Little Bunny, rubbing the bump on his head. "Maybe flying wasn't such a good idea after all."

The Telescope

It was a rainy day. It had poured down since breakfast time without a break. Little Bunny stared out of the window and sighed.

"I'm bored," said Benny, who was leaning on the windowsill beside him. "What shall we do?"

"I know," said Little Bunny, jumping up. "Why don't we go exploring?"

"We'd get wet," grumbled Benny.

"I don't mean *outside*. Let's explore *inside*. There are

lots and lots of passages leading from our burrow."

They wrapped some raisins and pumpkin seeds in a clean hanky and borrowed Daddy's torch to light their way.

The passage got dustier and narrower as they went along. After a few minutes Benny called out, "Look!" and he waved the torch up and down to show a door in the wall of the passage.

The handle was hard to turn, but with a bit of wiggling they managed it and the door creaked slowly open. Benny and Little Bunny could hardly see in the dark room, but they could just about make out the shapes of some chairs and boxes. As their eyes got used to the darkness, they began to see all sorts of other things—candlesticks, old paintings and bottles, a trombone and a

marble statue. Everything was covered in a thick layer of dust as though no one had been there for ages.

In a corner they found a big, wooden box with S. B. in gold letters on the lid. Inside were a lot of old maps and a shiny gold tube with glass ends.

"What do you think this is?" asked Benny, holding it up.

Little Bunny shook his head, "No idea. Let's ask Daddy."

Daddy was very pleased when they showed him the tube.

"I haven't seen that old thing for years!" he said. "It belonged to my grandfather, Silas Bunny. He was a sea captain and he sailed to lots of faraway places. I'll tell you all about his adventures one day."

"Oo, yes please," said Little Bunny. "But what *is* it?"

"It's a telescope. You look through one end and it makes things look bigger. Grandfather used it when he was at sea to search for land. You can use it at night, too, to see the stars. It's stopped raining now, so we could try it out later."

After tea, Mr Bunny told them an exciting story of how Silas Bunny sailed through a terrible storm. Then he took them outside to look at the stars through the telescope.

"They're beautiful," said Bunny. "I never notice them usually."

"Come on," said Mr Bunny. "Time for bed. We'll use the telescope another day."

"All right," said Little Bunny, yawning. "Isn't it funny how the worst days sometimes turn out to be the best?"

The Snow Dragon

One snowy day, Little Bunny, Little Mouse and Little Owl were looking at a picture book. It was full of stories about monsters and dragons.

"Do you think there are dragons in our wood?" asked Little Mouse.

"I don't know," said Little Bunny, "but we could go and look for one this afternoon. We'd see its tracks in the snow."

So, that afternoon, they wrapped up warmly in coats, scarves, gloves and wellington boots, before stepping out into the thick snow.

"Don't forget to look for tracks," Little Bunny told the others. They peered closely at every print they came across.

"That's Little Squirrel," said Little Mouse. "You can tell her by the brush marks that her tail makes in the snow."

They saw bunny tracks and fox tracks and prints made by birds —but nothing that looked like a dragon print.

"I'm getting cold," said Little Owl, running on ahead. "See you later!"

Little Mouse was getting cold too, and hoped that they could go home soon. "Perhaps dragons don't come out in the snow," she said hopefully.

Just then, as they turned a corner, Little Bunny pulled at Little Mouse's sleeve in excitement.

"Shh! There it is!" whispered Little Bunny, pointing to a strange track.

"It's a very big print," said Little Mouse. "I'm not sure I want to meet a dragon after all."

"Come on," said Little Bunny, and they followed the strange tracks deeper into the wood.

The prints led to a hollow tree.

"The dragon must be hiding in that tree," whispered Little Bunny. "Let's creep up from behind."

They crept up to the tree and peeped in. The dragon had its back to them. It wasn't big—in fact, it was quite small, and brown. Then it moved!

"Quick, it's coming!" whispered Little Mouse.

Little Bunny hid behind a bush, and Little Mouse hid behind Little Bunny—and they waited. Then Little Bunny started to giggle.

"It's Little Owl!" he shouted.

Little Owl came over to them, and they all laughed and laughed. On his feet he had tied bunches of leaves which left the strange marks in the snow.

"It was so cold looking for dragon prints that I thought I'd better make some myself," explained Little Owl.

"I'm very glad you did," said Little Mouse. "Now we can all go to my house for some hot chocolate."

"Hot chocolate," said Little Owl, "is a dragon's favourite drink!"

Little Squirrel Finds a Stone

Little Squirrel came running into the classroom. Late again. Mr Mole looked at his watch and frowned.

"Why are you so late, Little Squirrel?" whispered her friend, Timmy Mouse.

"I found a really beautiful stone," she explained.

"Let's see," whispered Timmy.

"I couldn't pick it up. It was stuck to the ground. I'll take you to see it at break-time."

When break-time came at last, Little Squirrel led Timmy—and Benny Bunny who was always nosey—to the stone.

"It's very shiny and it's got a pattern like a tortoise's shell," explained Little Squirrel. "It's over here."

"Where?" asked Timmy and Benny.

"Well it *was* here."

"Perhaps you made a mistake," suggested Timmy.

"No, I know it was beside that foxglove."

Just then Benny called out, "Over here!" and Little Squirrel and Timmy ran to the oak tree.

"Is that it?" asked Benny, pointing to a shiny stone.

"Yes, yes! That's it," said Little Squirrel. "But how did it move?"

"You just forgot where it was," said Benny and he tried to pick up the stone. "It *is* stuck to the ground."

"Let's tell Mr Mole about it," suggested Timmy.

Mr Mole listened and then said, "Hm. Most interesting. Shall we have a look?"

The whole class marched out to the oak tree, but the stone had gone. Mr Mole looked cross.

"I don't like silly jokes," he said. "I've a good mind to keep you in after school."

Then a bunny called, "Here it is!" and they all ran to look.

Mr Mole roared with laughter. "No wonder it keeps moving!" he said. "It's not a stone at all—it's Sammy Snail!"

The Egg-and-Spoon Race

School Sports Day was always good fun. There were lots of competitions but everybody's favourite was the egg-and-spoon race. Little Bunny was very good at running so he usually took home quite a few prizes, but he never won the egg-and-spoon race.

"My egg always falls off," he told Little Squirrel.

"Well, you just have to keep trying," said Little Squirrel kindly. "Stick at it."

"That's it!" shouted Little Bunny excitedly.

"What?" asked Little Squirrel, looking surprised.

"Oh, nothing," answered Little Bunny and he ran off home.

The next day was Sports Day. After the long-jump competition, which was won by Little Bunny, it was time for the egg-and-spoon race. The runners all lined up and Mr Mole shouted, "Go!"

They couldn't run very fast because they had to keep their eggs from falling off. Little Owl lost his almost at once, but Little Bunny seemed to run like the wind and finished well ahead of the others.

"I won! I won!" he shouted excitedly and he waved his spoon in the air.

"Careful!" called Mr Owl, who was standing at the finishing line. "If you wave your spoon like that the egg will drop off."

But Little Bunny didn't hear. He jumped up and down and

tossed his spoon up high and caught it. The egg was still on the spoon.

"Come here," said Mr Owl. "Let me look at that spoon."

He took the spoon and tried to lift the egg. He couldn't. It was glued on. Little Bunny went red.

Mr Mole marched over and told Little Bunny there would be no

prizes for him that day—not even for the other races he had won. Little Bunny went home with drooping ears.

"I'll never ever cheat again," he told Benny Bunny. "But I'll practise and practise so that next year I *will* win the egg-and-spoon race—properly!"

The Window-Cleaner

Mrs Bunny was in a flap. She was having a tea party that afternoon and the house was untidy. She was rushing round with her duster and broom saying, "Oh dear, oh dear, I'll never be ready in time."

She went outside to shake her duster and noticed how dirty the windows were.

"Just look at those windows!" she said. "Well, I've no time to clean them, so they'll have to stay dirty." She turned to Little Bunny and Benny, who were playing ball on the lawn. "Can't you be more careful?" she asked crossly. "I don't want the flowers all trampled down when my friends arrive for tea."

"Oh dear," said Benny. "I think we should go and play somewhere else while Mummy's in this mood."

"Good idea," said Little Bunny. "Let's go and see Mr Coggles."

Mr Coggles was an old rabbit who invented clever machines that did useful things—like sucking tea leaves out of drains or sticking labels on jam jars.

"Come in, come in," he said. "So pleased to see you!" He led them into his crowded little living room where there were machines of all shapes and sizes.

"I'm in the middle of inventing something at the moment," he told them. "You might be able to help me with it. You see, I don't know what to use it for. It was meant to be a shoe polisher, but the polish is too thick to squeeze through the tube."

He led the way to his workshop and showed them the machine. It looked like a mop with a hose leading from it to a bucket. There was a pump on the bucket for pumping the polish up the hose to the mop.

"It would work much better with water," said Little Bunny.

"Yes, yes, it would," agreed Mr Coggles.

"A window-cleaner!" shouted Benny excitedly.

"What?" asked Mr Coggles, looking round to see if someone had come to clean his windows.

"No," said Benny. "This machine is a window-cleaner. It's perfect!"

"Can we borrow it?" asked Little Bunny when he understood.

"Yes, of course," said Mr Coggles, looking a bit surprised.

Little Bunny and Benny raced home with the window-cleaner. Mrs Bunny was busy dusting the living room, so she didn't see

them filling the bucket at the kitchen tap. They crept outside and started the machine. The pump sent water up to the mop, which went round and round, polishing the windows until they shone.

When Mrs Bunny saw the windows she was very pleased and gave them both a piece of the shortbread she had just made for her tea party.

"Let's take the machine back to Mr Coggles," said Benny.

Mr Coggles was very excited to hear how well it worked.

"Splendid! Splendid!" he said. "You know, it wasn't really me who invented it. If you two hadn't come up with the window-cleaner idea I don't know what I would have done. I'd like you to keep it."

"Thanks, Mr Coggles!" said Little Bunny.

From that day on the Bunnies' house had the cleanest, shiniest windows in the whole village!

The Nature Lesson

"In our next Nature Study lesson we're going to talk about trees," said Mr Mole. "Tomorrow I'd like you all to bring in something that comes from a tree."

The next morning they all trooped in with their finds. Little Squirrel brought an acorn, Timmy Mouse had a big golden sycamore leaf, Benny Bunny brought an oak apple and Little Bunny had a caterpillar that lived on leaves.

Mr Mole looked at all their things one by one, but by the time he got to Little Bunny, the caterpillar had crawled away.

"Oh dear, where is it?" wailed Little Bunny.

Then Timmy screamed. "Aah! Something's tickling my back!"

It was Little Bunny's caterpillar!

"I think we'd better take it outside," said Mr Mole, carefully lifting it off Timmy's back.

Then he turned to Little Owl, who had nothing at all.

"What have you to show us?" asked Mr Mole. "I can't see anything."

"Me!" said Little Owl. "*I* come from a tree!"

The Expedition

"Let's go on an expedition!" said Little Bunny to Nippy Shrew one morning.

"What does it mean?" asked Nippy. "An exper . . . whatsit?"

"Um . . . an adventure—a long journey to find something."

"What are we looking for?" asked Nippy, feeling puzzled.

"I don't know. We'll just see what we find."

Off they went through the bluebell glade, over the mossy

mound and into the beech wood.

"We haven't found anything yet," complained Nippy, whose legs were aching.

"Well you don't *always* find things on expeditions," said Little Bunny. "Why don't we stop and have a rest?" He turned to Nippy—but there was no one behind him. "Nippy, where are you? Nippy! Stop playing games!"

"I'm down here!" said Nippy's faint and faraway voice.

"Where?" shouted Little Bunny, looking round.

Hidden in the bracken by the edge of the path was a large hole. At the bottom of the hole was Nippy.

"How did you get down there?" asked Little Bunny.

"I fell, silly!" said Nippy, crossly.

There was no way out. The sides were steep and straight. Little Bunny tried reaching down, but it was no good. The hole was too deep.

"I'll have to fetch a rope," said Little Bunny. "I'll be as quick as I can. You stay there."

Nippy didn't have much choice!

When Little Bunny got back he was surprised to find Nippy looking so cheerful after such a long wait. He lowered the rope and pulled him safely out of the hole.

"What are you smiling for?" he asked.

"It's been a good expedition after all," explained Nippy. "You see, I *have* found something. It was at the bottom of the hole." In his hand he held a shiny silver coin. "We've enough here to buy all the liquorice we can eat and some marbles too!"

The Bunnies' Christmas Party

The Bunnies were giving a Christmas party. They had asked all their friends and Little Bunny and Benny had put up holly and paper chains to make the house seem bright and cheerful.

Mrs Bunny came in to see how everything looked.

"Lovely!" she said. "All we need to do now is decorate the Christmas tree."

Little Bunny and Benny wanted to do that. They hung tinsel from the branches and then added some shiny bells and a big silver star.

"We're ready to put the lights on," called Little Bunny and Mrs Bunny brought in the box of Christmas lights. She wrapped them carefully round the tree—but when she pressed the switch, nothing happened!

"I expect there's a loose one," said Mr Bunny and he checked

each light to make sure. They still didn't work.

"It's such a shame when we're having a party," said Mrs Bunny. "There must be something we can do."

"I've got an idea," said Little Bunny, running to the door. "I won't be long!"

"I wonder what he's doing," said Mrs Bunny a little later. "I hope he gets back soon or everyone will be here before him."

Just then the door opened and in came Little Bunny.

"I've brought some new guests," he said. "Come in, everyone!"

Ten little glow worms wiggled their way into the house.

"They'll make perfect Christmas tree lights," said Little Bunny, helping the glow worms to climb onto the branches.

The glow worms really enjoyed themselves and all the party guests thought they looked very pretty. Soon they were being invited to decorate Christmas trees in houses all over Hollyholt and they found themselves at parties every night!